Death at
Owls Gate

Death at Owls Gate

Nathan Dolan

Copyright © 2023 Nathan Dolan

Paperback: ISBN 9798385535781

Edited by Matt Dolan

Owls Gate

In the dark streets of London, a figure approached Owls Gate. The figure was tall and thin, with a gleaming blade by his side.

Owls Gate is the home of Lord Theodore Monrow and Colin Monrow. The house is large and white with tall black gates.

The figure approached the house, the tall gates trembled in the wind, the figure climbed them and silently walked across the gravel path.

The man shattered the living room window and climbed in. He went up the long winding staircase. It creaked under his feet. Finally, he got to his target, and gently pushed the door open. The man took out something that glinted in the moonlight. Suddenly, a scream echoed around the house!

As the sun rose, Colin woke, his four-poster bed creaking as he got up. He got dressed and went down the long winding staircase. In his kitchen, Colin sat down at the polished birch table. He looked around. Colin could not see his father.

He got up and went to his father's room—the door was open and a cold breeze came through it. Colin crept inside.

As he opened the door he felt a sharp pain in his heart—his father was lying motionless on the bed, a knife in his torso, scarlet blood dripping off the bed.

The Case

Two months later…

"Detective Colin, come here now!" shouted Tom, Colin's boss, "I have another case for you. How did your father die?"

The next day, Colin went to go and find out who killed his father.

Hesitantly, Colin entered Owls Gate; he had left his father's room in the same state as the day he died. As Colin nervously opened the large oak doors, a gush of unpleasant smell filled his nostrils.

Colin looked for any clues. He looked by the window, in the cupboard, and under the bed where he discovered a tattered, old, black cloak.

At the detective headquarters, Colin gave the cloak to Tom. "Good work, Colin." beamed Tom. He took the cloak and put it on the desk beside him, as they both left for the night.

Colin woke up with a start. It was hammering down with rain, and great big zig-zags danced through the sky. He drifted back to sleep, the sounds of the storm filling his room.

That morning, Colin could smell the smoky stench of burning. He rushed down the stairs. Colin could see dazzling flames dancing about the room with tails of smoke floating above his head.

Hot gushes of air burnt his face, the flames spoke to each other in crackling voices. Colin fought desperately to put them out and eventually won.

Later that day, Colin reluctantly walked to work. When he got there, Colin was surprised to see that Tom was absent.

Colin could hear a noisy rustling sound under Tom's desk. He bent down.

Under the desk was a trap door. Colin curiously pushed away the desk and opened the trap door…

The Trap Door

Colin anxiously lowered himself through the trap door. He landed in an empty tunnel. It smelt damp and earthy, water dripping from the ceiling. The floor was wet and sticky, Colin could see the faint outline of rats running along the floor.

As Colin walked, bones cracked ominously under his feet.

Eventually, the tunnel widened into a room.

Colin saw a box of matches and some wood lying on the floor next to a long black cloak. The cloak was dusty, ripped and smelt of blood.

Colin turned around and saw a small fireplace with a chair facing it; a gloomy picture hung above the fireplace. As he passed the chair, something or someone on it moved.

Colin's stomach tightened.

Somehow he knew this was a person he didn't want to meet.

He ran through the nearest exit, onwards further into the tunnel.

Hundreds of metres later, Colin was breathless and sweat poured down his face. He looked around, seeing that he wasn't followed. Looking down, he was shocked to see a puddle of dark red blood stained the stone floor.

A knife lay in the centre of the pool. It had a leather handle with T.N. engraved on it.

Further down the tunnel, Colin could see a light spilling into the gloom. He rushed out, and found himself in a dark alleyway, surrounded by hissing cats.

He ran on, afraid of what could be
behind him until eventually, he found
his way home.

Back at Owl's Gate, Colin's mind was
racing. "Why is that knife there and
who is T.N?"

Colin thought for a while An idea
gradually formed in his head.

The Box

"Are you feeling okay Colin?" Sam asked anxiously.

Sam and Colin had known each other since school.

"Oh, I'm fine."

Colin and Sam were walking in Battersea Park. Towering oak trees were bending over the narrow mud path, the trees whispered to each other as if they were telling secrets.

Later, when Colin got home he rushed up to his bedroom.

Colin had a box under his bed, containing pictures of his dad and things he had done.

Hunting through the box, Colin eventually found the paper he was looking for: a coffee-stained sheet of A4 with large, scruffy handwriting scribbled along the margin.

At the break of dawn, Colin raced to HQ. At his desk, he put down the paper and started working.

When the clock struck midnight, Colin looked out of the window; the sky was dark blue with white stars sprinkled all over it.

Outside, Colin could see a battered car parked by the road, with a man sitting inside.

Without wasting a moment, Colin darted out of the back door. He ran and ran, until his lungs screamed with pain.

He could hear a horrible voice not far behind calling out, "Come on, Colin! Come on."

Colin finally got to the gates of his house. He slammed them behind him, just in time, and turned to look.

The man stood just the other side of the gates. He was so close that Colin could feel his cold, rasping breath against his face.

Colin could just about make out the man's face in the dim light. It was dark and grim, a deep cut running down his cheek.

He looked like Tom!

"T.N. — Tom Night! It all made sense now — the knife, the fire and the box," muttered Colin.

"You murdered my father!" Colin shouted, his voice ringing.

The Telephone

"So, what happened again?" Sam asked.

Sam and Colin were talking upstairs in Sam's bedroom. Sam's record player was going round and round.

"Can you turn that thing off! I can't concentrate," Colin complained.

"So, what's the box?" Sam asked.

"It's a box of all the things my dad did," Colin replied.

"What did your dad do?" Sam asked.

"Well, he killed Hitler," Colin replied, a bit angry at Sam's question.

"But I thought Hitler killed himself," Sam muttered.

"No—that's what everyone thinks, but it's not true!" said Colin.

When the sun had risen, Colin looked out the window. It was a sunny day, and the air smelt pleasant, with the familiar fragrance of mud and grass.

As he left his house, closing the front door behind him, Colin thought about how he would get the evidence for his father's murder. He walked down the road.

Passing a telephone box, he had the best idea —he could call the police!

Colin dialled 999. While he was dialling, a man crept unseen behind the phone box...

"Hello, who is this?" the operator asked.

"This is Colin Monrow from the detective HQ in London."

"What evidence would you like to submit?" the voice questioned.

Ten minutes later…

"And your address please?"

All the talking had worn Colin out. He put down the phone and tried to open the door. It wouldn't budge!

Colin could see a figure striding away from the telephone box. "Let me out! Let me out!"

Out of the corner of his eye, Colin saw a rock just outside the phone box. He manoeuvred his hand through a crack in the glass and picked the rock up, his hand shaking. SMASH! The noise of the glass shattering made the nearby birds scatter.

Colin climbed through the hole, ripping his clothes and lacerating his skin as he did. He wandered home, a few drops of blood dripping from his arms.

The following morning, Colin sat at his table eating toast. Suddenly, a letter tumbled through the letterbox. Picking up the envelope, Colin wondered who it was from.

Ripping open the flap, he read the contents:

Dear Mr Colin Monrow,

Your information has been received. We can send you a police car to pick up the criminal. He will be sent to court on Friday.

From the head of police in Scotland

Colin's face lit up, he was so relieved.

Catching Tom

Friday: Colin woke up, he jumped out of bed. "Time to catch Tom Night!"

Colin walked down the gravel path, a police van waiting on the road. Colin got in, started the engine and put his foot on the accelerator.

Passing an alleyway, he spotted a man and quickly turned into the alleyway. The man froze. Colin got out and looked at the man's face—not Tom.

Back in his van, he passed another man. He leapt out—also not Tom.

Driving around the streets, he finally saw him in the distance. Colin found a pair of handcuffs in the van.

Colin quietly stopped the van, got out, and silently snuck up behind the man.

Colin grabbed Tom's arm and tried to put the handcuffs on him but Tom ran.

Colin chased after him.

They both raced till they got to a park. Colin grabbed Tom's hand and cuffed him. He dragged Tom back to the van and shoved him in.

Colin walked through the large oak doors of the court pulling Tom Night along. The judge sat on the bench. Colin placed Tom in the dock and sat himself in the well.

The trial took minutes.

Before long, the judge pronounced, "I sentence you to prison for murder!"

As Tom was marched out of the court doors, he caught Colin's eye, a look of anger on his face.

"Goodnight, Tom," Colin said with a smirk.

"Or should I say, *bad* Night!"

About the Author

Nathan Dolan was born on 22nd of September 2002 in Sydney, Australia. At the age of 10, Nathan went to St. Cuthbert's school, where he found his love for writing.

He moved to England on 8th of June 2019. He started writing novels in 2021. In 2022 he set a world record for the longest novel typed by foot.

Nathan enjoys writing fictional About the Author sections for his books.

Have you read:

The Silver Blade

Theo B.R

Printed in Great Britain
by Amazon